THE ICE PALACE

by Angela McAllister

illustrated by Angela Barrett

G. P. Putnam's Sons

It was the hottest season in a hot, dry land.

Anna was unwell. Her mother made a bed in the little garden room, and her father laid her gently down.

"When the cool winds come they will find you here," he promised. But the cool winds didn't come.

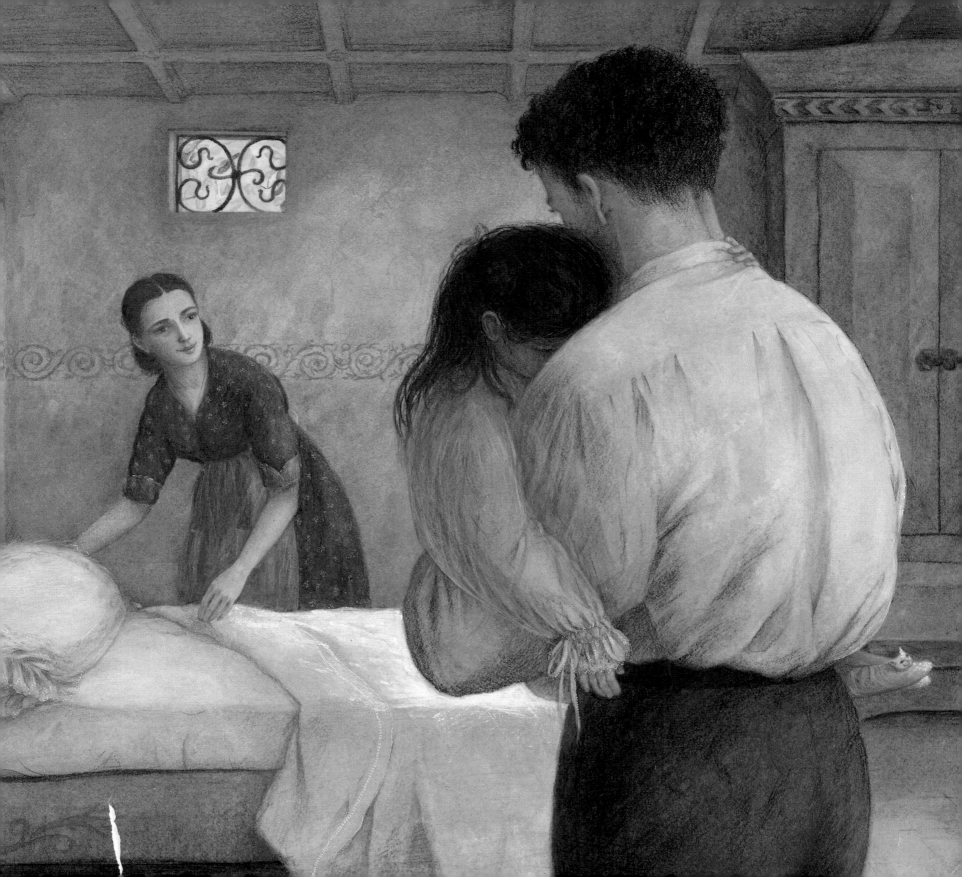

All day Anna lay, drowsy in the heat. Outside lazy lizards baked in the sun and lemons ripened on the trees.

Anna watched the white palace on the hill glisten, like a pearl set in the mountains. And she watched the ice house.

Anna's father worked in the palace kitchens.

When he came home that evening he bathed her hot hands.

"I have been asked to prepare a surprise for the grand banquet table," he said, "but it is a secret I cannot tell."

"Then tell me a story," asked Anna.

And so her father told her a story about the snow-white mountains, where the North Wind blusters through his icy halls.

"The cool winds will come soon, Anna," he promised as he said good night. "Now go to sleep."

But Anna watched the stars awhile. She saw four men pass with great sacks.

And the sacks seemed to overflow with diamonds that sparkled in the moonlight. They took them to the ice house.

Then Anna slept and dreamt she was flying with the North Wind through his mountain chambers . . .

The next day Anna's fever was worse. Her mother made paper fans and hung them around the little garden room, but there was no breeze to move them.

Anna watched the lizards and the lemons. And she watched the ice house.

When her father came home that evening he bathed her hot head. But still he would not tell his secret.

"Then tell me a story," asked Anna.

So her father told her a story about a land where snowflakes always fell. And there lived a princess in an ice palace, where all the rooms were hung with icicles.

"Your fever will soon pass, Anna," he promised as he said good night. "Now go to sleep."

But Anna listened to the nightbirds awhile. She saw her father slip between the lemon trees with his lantern. He went into the ice house.

Then Anna slept and dreamt she was a princess, dancing through her palace of ice, in a dress made of snowflakes . . .

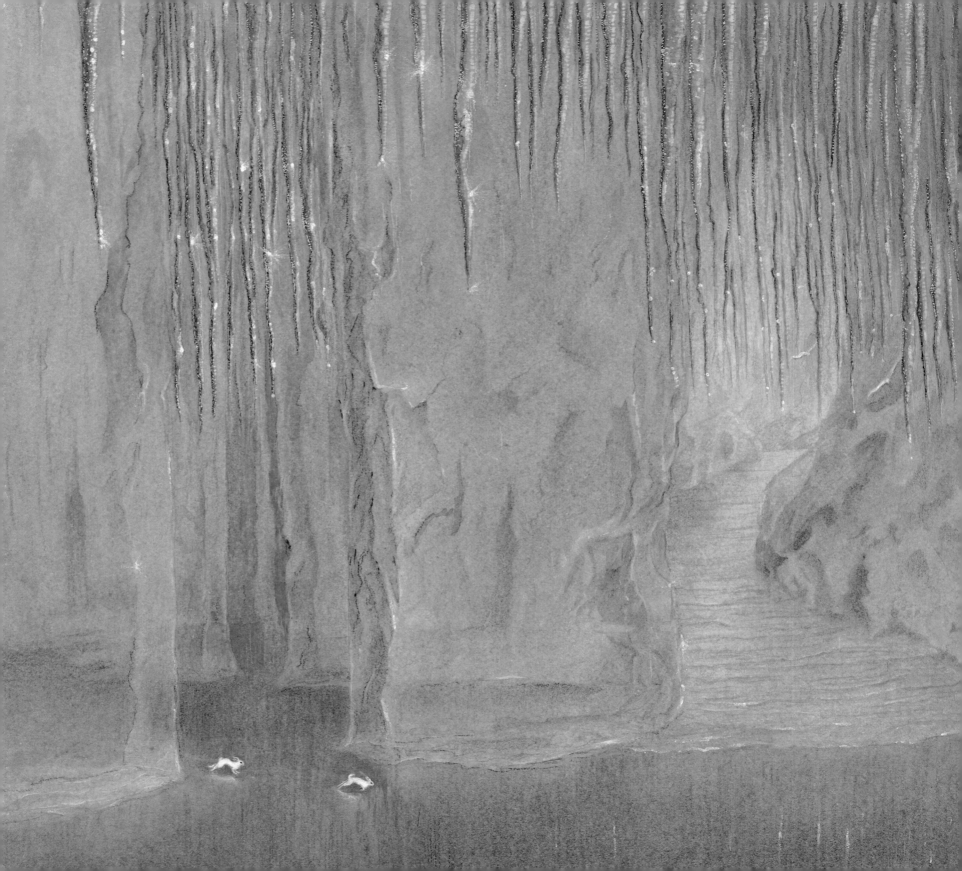

The next day Anna was still weak with fever. The sun burned down.

"That old sun is trying to melt the world," said her mother. And she brought a jug of sweet fruit juices.

Anna watched the lizards dart in the shadows, and she heard the lemons drop to the ground. And she watched the ice house.

When her father came home that evening he bathed her hot arms. But he would not tell his secret.

"Then tell me a story," asked Anna.

So he told her a story about the land of white bears, where a frozen river hung over a silent waterfall, above a still, crystal lake, where ice ships with silken sails were held fast, never to sail free.

"You will soon be well again, Anna," he promised as he said good night. "Now go to sleep."

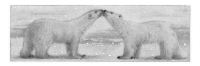

But Anna watched the moon awhile. Once more she saw her father's lantern glow among the lemon trees as he made his way to the ice house.

   Then she slept and dreamt she was raising the billowing blue sails of her ice ship, as snowbirds circled around the masts . . .

The next day Anna was too weak to open her eyes. Her mother sat by the window, making baskets to sell at the market.

"If only I could throw a basket high enough to catch a breeze." She sighed. "But a breeze cannot be caught."

The heat lay like a great blanket, so warm and heavy that the world was still. Outside the sun scorched the lizards and the lemons. And it burnt down on the ice house.

When Anna's father came home that evening he gently bathed her hot eyelids. But he would not tell his secret.

"Then tell me a story," she asked.

So he told her the story of how the North Wind roared from his mountain chambers into the princess's palace, shattering all the icicles with a great crash. And she fled along the bank of the white river, down to the frozen lake where her ice ship was waiting. Then a flock of snowbirds pulled the ship slowly until the ice began to crack and the ship was free.

"Now go to sleep," said her father, as he had no more promises.

And Anna slept. She didn't see her father make his way once more to the ice house.

That night Anna dreamt she was a princess, chased through the mountains by the North Wind. She escaped on a great ice ship, with blue silk sails, and was pulled by snowbirds through a frozen lake out to the wide blue sea.

Anna opened her eyes.

She saw blue sails sway above her head and heard the wind rustle. A cool breeze soothed her warm cheek. And, when she stretched out her fingers, Anna felt the frozen chill of ice.

There before her was the most beautiful ship, carved in ice, sparkling like a diamond. It had tall, fine masts and sails, and a prow in the shape of a snowbird.

"The breeze has blown your fever away," said her father. "And here is my secret for you."

Anna felt well again. She held the ice ship up to the window of the little garden room. The sun sent rainbows through it. "That old sun would like to melt your secret." She laughed.

But Anna's father knew what to do. Gently he lifted her up and carried her out, past the lazy lizards, between the lemon trees to the ice house.

With a rusty key he unlocked the door and they stepped inside. The ice house sparkled like a crystal cave.

There where the hot sun would never find it, they set Anna's ice ship in the heart of its frozen lake.

And once more, Anna was the princess in her ice palace.

For Mark,
who makes everything possible—A.M.

For my dear family—A.B.

Before refrigerators were invented, palaces had ice houses.
They were built at least partly underground, often from brick,
and were well insulated from the sun's rays.
Ice could be stored in them all year round.

G. P. Putnam's Sons, a division of The Putnam & Grosset Group,
200 Madison Avenue, New York, NY 10016
G. P. Putnam's Sons, Reg. U.S. Pat. & Tm. Off.
Simultaneously published in Great Britain by Hutchinson Children's Books,
Random House UK Limited, London. Published simultaneously in Canada.
Printed in Singapore. Text set in Perpetua.

Library of Congress Cataloging-in-Publication Data
McAllister, Angela.   The ice palace / by Angela McAllister;
illustrated by Angela Barrett.—1st American ed.   p.   cm.
"Simultaneously published in Great Britain by Hutchinson Children's Books . . . London"—T.p. verso.
Summary: While Anna lies sick with a fever, her father tells her stories about an ice palace
in a land of icy cold and plans a marvelous surprise for her.
[1. Ice—Fiction. 2. Cold—Fiction. 3. Heat—Fiction. 4. Sick—Fiction.] I. Barrett, Angela, ill.
II. Title.   PZ7.M47825Ic   1994   [E]—dc20   93-45255   CIP   AC
ISBN 0-399-22784-9
1   3   5   7   9   10   8   6   4   2

First American Edition

E
MCA

McAllister, Angela.
The ice palace.

20648

$15.95

DATE			

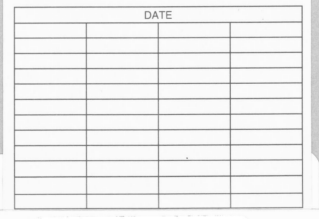